Where's Al?

Byron Barton

Clarion Books/New York

 L.C. Catalog Card Number: 78-171866. ISBN: 0-395-28765-0 PA ISBN 0-395-51582-3
(Previously published by the Seabury Press under ISBN: 0-8164-3088-8) Printed in China WKT 15 14 13
Clarion Books / a Houghton Mifflin Company imprint / 215 Park Avenue South, New York, NY 10003

AL!

Where's Al?

Al is lost.

Fru

I'm not hungry.

I can't sleep.

I'll find Al today.

sanitation

LOST
DOG
REWARD

Did you find a dog?

Lost dog
reward
200 3rd av

ts
Vegetab
I Lost my dog.

hot dogs

Sanitation

Fruits
Veget

hot dogs
Did you see a dog?

Fruits

hot dogs
sanitation

Ruff !

hot dogs
Sanitation

Fruits
AL!

Lost dog